Ruth and the Green Book

For the inspiration and impetus for this book, I am forever indebted to Little Tony and his family.
—C.A.R.

For my Ruth.
—F.C.

Story concept by Janice Shea, Pinafore Press

Carolrhoda Books
A division of Lerner Publishing Group, Inc.
241 First Avenue North
Minneapolis, MN 55401 U.S.A.

Website address: www.lernerbooks.com

The following images are used with the permission of: From the Collections of The Henry Ford (87.135.1736), p. 32 (both).

Library of Congress Cataloging-in-Publication Data

Ramsey, Calvin A.
Ruth and the Green Book / by Calvin Alexander Ramsey ; illustrated by Floyd Cooper.
p. cm.
Summary: When Ruth and her parents take a motor trip from Chicago to Alabama to visit her grandma, they rely on a pamphlet called "The Negro Motorist Green Book" to find places that will serve them. Includes facts about "The Green Book."
ISBN: 978-0-7613-5255-6 (lib. bdg. : alk. paper)
[1. Segregation—Fiction. 2. African Americans—Fiction. 3. Automobile travel—Fiction. 4. Southern States—History—20th century—Fiction.] I. Cooper, Floyd, ill. II. Title.
PZ7.R145Ru 2010
[E]—dc22 2009034284

Manufactured in the United States of America
1 – VI – 7/15/10

Ruth and the Green Book

Calvin Alexander Ramsey
with Gwen Strauss
illustrations by Floyd Cooper

Carolrhoda Books
Minneapolis

It was a BIG day at our house when Daddy drove up in our very own automobile—a 1952 Buick! It is the most beautiful color. Daddy calls it Sea Mist Green.

He bought it for his new job, but first, we planned to go on a trip to visit Grandma in Alabama.

I was so excited to travel across the country! I packed my own bag, and Mama said I could take Brown Bear with me for company, even though I'm almost too old for him.

As we drove out of Chicago,
it felt funny to see the neighborhood disappear
and then the streets and then the buildings.

I love all the green grass and hills and trees. Daddy told lots of stories about when he was a boy in Alabama. He made us laugh.

Eventually, we stopped and had a picnic lunch that Mama had packed. She had been cooking all week to get ready for the trip.

RESTROOM

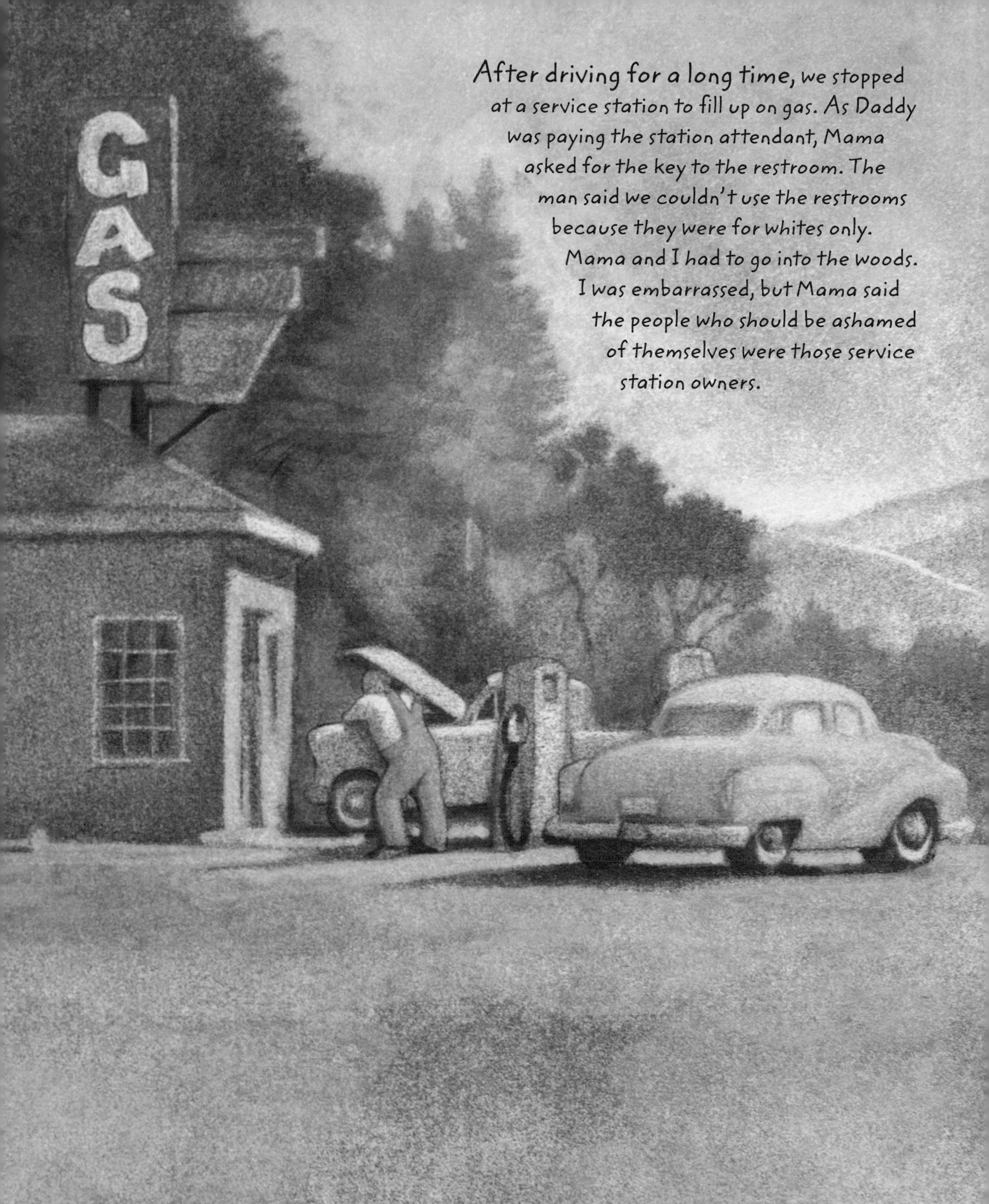

After driving for a long time, we stopped at a service station to fill up on gas. As Daddy was paying the station attendant, Mama asked for the key to the restroom. The man said we couldn't use the restrooms because they were for whites only. Mama and I had to go into the woods. I was embarrassed, but Mama said the people who should be ashamed of themselves were those service station owners.

I was tired when Daddy stopped the automobile. I asked Mama where we were, and she said we were going to spend the night in a real hotel. We watched Daddy talking to the man behind the desk. Daddy was smiling and pointing to us. But the man shook his head and turned his back.

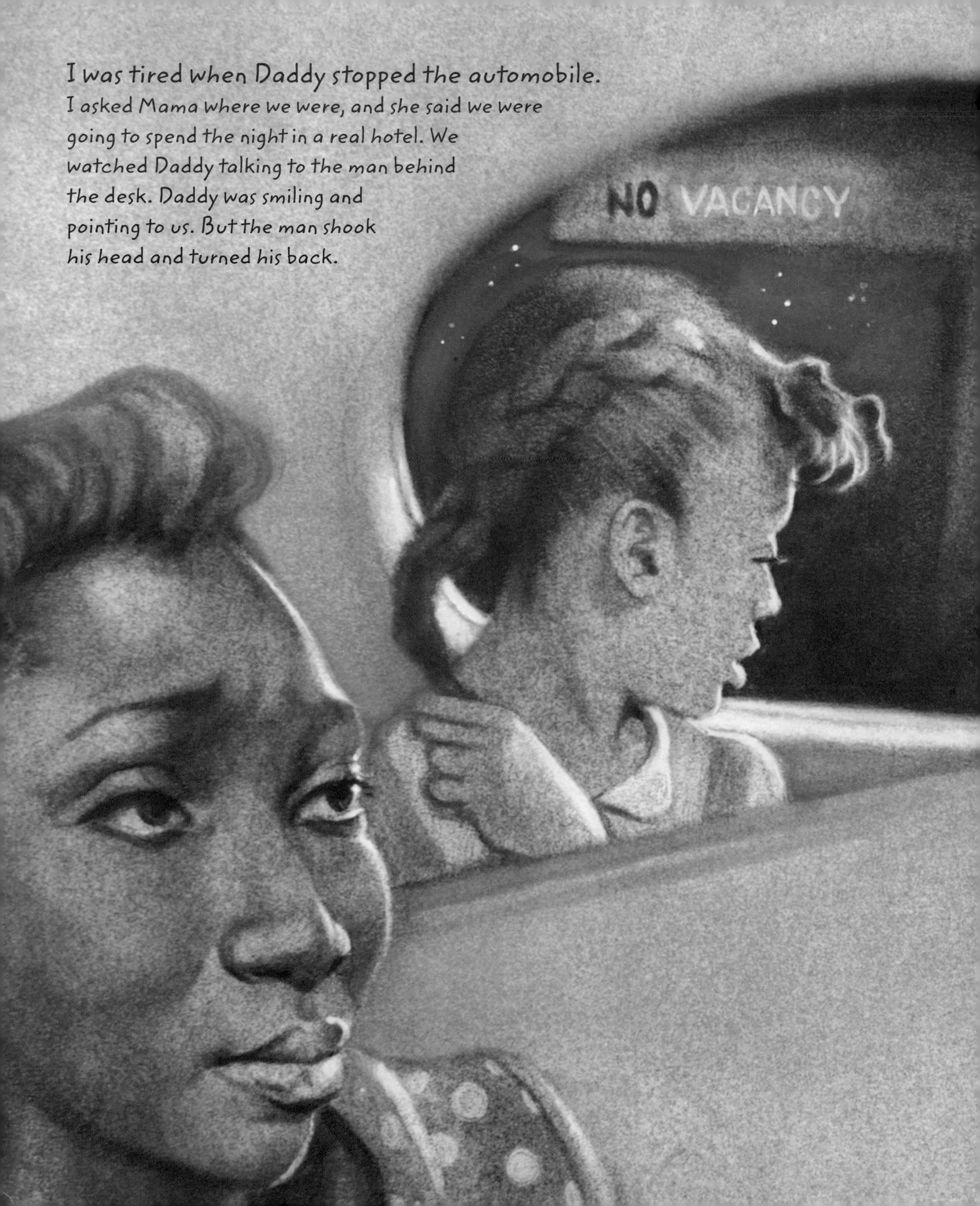

Daddy came back out and slammed the car door. He never slammed the door before, so I knew he was mad. I wondered what happened, but I knew somehow it wasn't a good time to ask him. Mama gave me a look that said, "Ruth, just keep quiet." So that's what I did.

We kept on driving through the night. Mama took a turn so Daddy could sleep. I fell asleep with Brown Bear as my pillow. We must have pulled off the road in the middle of the night, because when I woke in the morning, we were all curled up in the car. I was stiff and hungry. Mama gave us cold biscuits and jam for breakfast. She said we should sing to cheer ourselves up.

We sang a lot that day as we crossed the country. We had picnics at roadside stops for lunch and dinner because all the restaurants had signs in the windows that said we couldn't eat there. It seemed like there were "White Only" signs everywhere outside of our Chicago neighborhood. I felt homesick, and I hugged Brown Bear close all day.

When we crossed into Tennessee, Daddy said his friend, Eddy, lived close by. He was sure we could sleep there.

Eddy was so happy to see us! He gave me a big hug and told me that he knew me when I was real little. His wife, Alice, cooked us a warm meal, and I ate too much. Daddy and Eddy used to play music in a band before they went off and fought in the war. They talked about how they traveled a lot back then and how they always had a hard time finding places to rest and eat. Daddy shook his head and said he had hoped that the war had changed things, but now he could see he was wrong.

That night I went to sleep to the sound of Daddy and Eddy playing music together. Brown Bear and I were happy to sleep in a real bed with a real pillow.

The next day as we loaded the car, I heard Eddy talking quietly to Mama and Daddy. Eddy warned them about what was ahead, someone called Jim Crow. I heard Eddy tell them that however bad it was so far, it was only going to get worse for us, maybe even dangerous, as we went farther south. Then Eddy saw me listening, and he picked me up and told me not to worry. He said that I should look out for Esso service stations along the road, because the people there would be nice to us.

In the car, I asked Daddy who Jim Crow was, and he explained that "Jim Crow" wasn't a who. It was a bunch of ugly laws forbidding blacks and whites from mixing in any way. I asked, "Why don't they want our business? Wasn't our money just the same?" It hurt my feelings to be so unwelcome. But Mama sighed and reminded me that my job that day was to look for an Esso station.

Esso
Esso

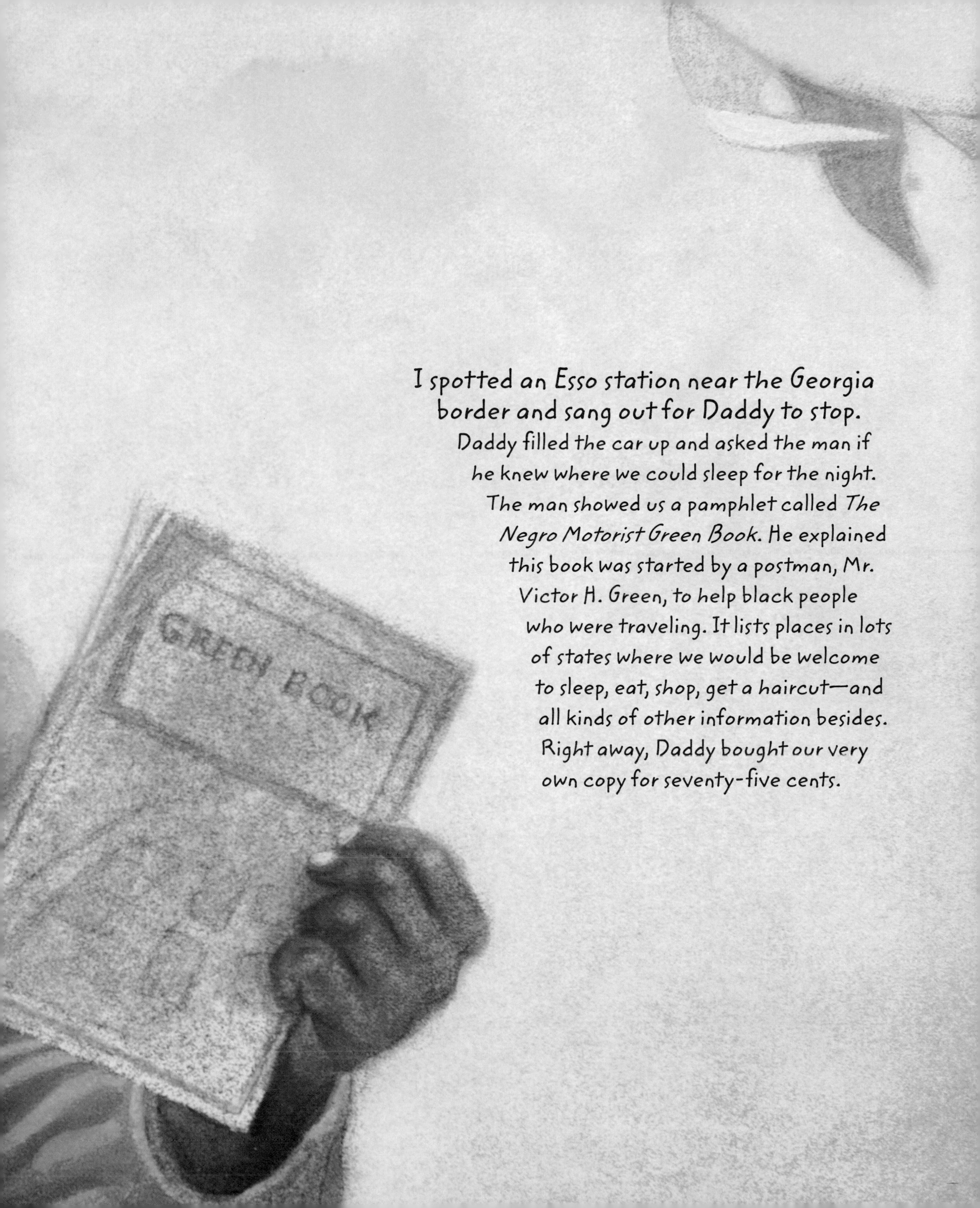

I spotted an Esso station near the Georgia border and sang out for Daddy to stop.

Daddy filled the car up and asked the man if he knew where we could sleep for the night. The man showed us a pamphlet called *The Negro Motorist Green Book*. He explained this book was started by a postman, Mr. Victor H. Green, to help black people who were traveling. It lists places in lots of states where we would be welcome to sleep, eat, shop, get a haircut—and all kinds of other information besides. Right away, Daddy bought our very own copy for seventy-five cents.

Mama read about a place nearby called a "tourist home" where we could stay for the last night of our trip. Daddy called ahead and sure enough, the lady told us to come right away. Then Mama gave me the Green Book and said I was in charge of keeping it. I couldn't stop reading it—all those places in all those states where we could go and not worry about being turned away.

We reached the tourist home in the early evening. Mrs. Melody, the owner, gave us a big smile when she opened the door. It was like coming home. And she wouldn't even let Daddy pay her. She said she welcomed Negro travelers because it was right to help each other out. I'm going to do the same one day!

The next morning, I hated to say good-bye to Mrs. Melody. But Daddy said we could be at Grandma's house that evening. That made me happy to get going again!

It wasn't so easy, though. Our automobile broke down about midday, in the middle of nowhere. People drove right past. I felt empty in the pit of my stomach. I hugged Brown Bear and wished we were already at Grandma's house. But Mama said not to worry, we could figure this out. She unfolded our map and told me the names of nearby towns. She said, "Ruth, look in the Green Book and see if you can find a place in one of these towns that will fix our car."

And I did! Daddy gave me a big hug, and then he walked into town to find the garage that would help us.

By the time we got the car fixed, it was too late to reach Grandma's house that day. So I looked in the Green Book and picked out an inn nearby that said they welcomed Negro travelers. It was a big house with lots of rooms. Most of the people there were businessmen traveling for their jobs. They each carried a Green Book. They said they could never do their jobs without it!

We met a salesman named Jason who has traveled to all the states of the Union for his job. He told such funny stories. Mama laughed so hard, she had tears rolling down her face. For the first time since we left home, we were really happy.

At the inn, I met a little boy who was traveling with his mother. It was the first time he had ever left home, and I could just tell he was scared. I thought of Mrs. Melody, Victor Green, Eddy, and all the other people who had helped us, and then I decided to give Brown Bear to the boy.

I told him that Brown Bear was a good traveler. I'm too old for Brown Bear now, and the little boy needed him more than I do. Then I told his mother about the Green Book and showed her our copy.

That night, before I went to sleep, I thought about our trip. It was not what I had expected—traveling could be scary, that's for sure! It made me sad that some people were mean to Negroes.

But it helped to know that good black people all over the country had pitched in to help each other. It felt like I was part of one big family! Plus, tomorrow I would finally see Grandma and tell her what a great Green Book guide I had been.

The History of *The Negro Motorist Green Book*

Decades after the Emancipation Proclamation and the Thirteenth Amendment ended slavery, African Americans continued to suffer unequal treatment, especially in the South, where Jim Crow laws discriminated against blacks in nearly every aspect of public life, including travel. Although the roads and highways were free for all to use, doing so was not easy for blacks. Most hotels and restaurants would not serve African Americans, and driving overnight often meant sleeping in cars and packing food to eat during the journey. Many gas stations would not sell gas to black drivers, so they had to carry gas cans and always be on the lookout for the few stations that would welcome their business. Even then, they might not be allowed to use a public restroom.

In 1936, an African American living in New York City named Victor Green wrote a book to help black travelers. He made a list of all the hotels, restaurants, gas stations, and businesses that would serve African Americans in his city. There was such a high demand for his book that he decided his next edition would include other towns in other states, as well.

The Green Book was sold for a quarter in 1940 at black-owned businesses and at Esso stations, which were among the only gas stations that sold to African Americans. Esso was owned by the Standard Oil Company, which eventually provided funding and offices for Victor Green. The Green Book quickly became very popular and helped many businessmen on the road, as well as the families who needed and wanted to travel by car.

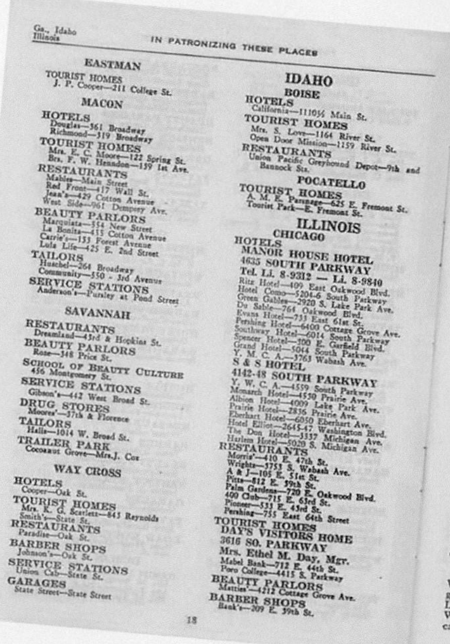

Ga., Idaho
Illinois

IN PATRONIZING THESE PLACES

EASTMAN

TOURIST HOMES
J. P. Cooper—211 College St.

MACON

HOTELS
Douglas—361 Broadway
Richmond—319 Broadway
TOURIST HOMES
Mrs. E. C. Moore—122 Spring St.
Bro. F. W. Henndon—139 1st Ave.
RESTAURANTS
Mables—Main Street
Red Front—417 Wall St.
Jean's—429 Cotton Avenue
West Side—961 Dempsey Ave.
BEAUTY PARLORS
Marquiata—554 New Street
La Bonita—415 Cotton Avenue
Carrie's—153 Forest Avenue
Lula Life—425 E. 2nd Street
TAILORS
Huschel—264 Broadway
Community—550 - 3rd Avenue
SERVICE STATIONS
Anderson's—Pursley at Pond Street

SAVANNAH

RESTAURANTS
Dreamland—43rd & Hopkins St.
BEAUTY PARLORS
Rose—348 Price St.
SCHOOL OF BEAUTY CULTURE
456 Montgomery St.
SERVICE STATIONS
Gibson's—442 West Broad St.
DRUG STORES
Moores'—37th & Florence
TAILORS
Halls—1014 W. Broad St.
TRAILER PARK
Cocoanut Grove—Mrs. J. Cox

WAY CROSS

HOTELS
Cooper—Oak St.
TOURIST HOMES
Mrs. K. G. Scatlett—845 Reynolds
Smith's—State St.
RESTAURANTS
Paradise—Oak St.
BARBER SHOPS
Johnson's—Oak St.
SERVICE STATIONS
Union Cab—State St.
GARAGES
State Street—State Street

IDAHO

BOISE

HOTELS
California—1110½ Main St.
TOURIST HOMES
Mrs. S. Love—1164 River St.
Open Door Mission—1159 River St.
RESTAURANTS
Union Pacific Greyhound Depot—9th and Bannock Sts.

POCATELLO

TOURIST HOMES
A. M. E. Parsonage—625 E. Fremont St.
Tourist Park—E. Fremont St.

ILLINOIS

CHICAGO

HOTELS
MANOR HOUSE HOTEL
4635 SOUTH PARKWAY
Tel. Li. 8-9312 — Li. 8-9840
Ritz Hotel—409 East Oakwood Blvd.
Hotel Como—5204-6 South Parkway
Green Gables—2920 S. Lake Park Ave.
Du Sable—764 Oakwood Blvd.
Evans Hotel—733 East 61st St.
Pershing Hotel—6400 Cottage Grove Ave.
Southway Hotel—6014 South Parkway
Spencer Hotel—300 E. Garfield Blvd.
Grand Hotel—5044 South Parkway
Y. M. C. A.—3763 Wabash Ave.
S & S HOTEL
4142-48 SOUTH PARKWAY
Y. W. C. A.—4559 South Parkway
Monarch Hotel—4550 Prairie Ave.
Albion Hotel—4009 Lake Park Ave.
Prairie Hotel—2836 Prairie Ave.
Eberhart Hotel—6050 Eberhart Ave.
Hotel Elliot—2645-47 Washington Blvd.
The Don Hotel—3337 Michigan Ave.
Harlem Hotel—5029 S. Michigan Ave.
RESTAURANTS
Morris'—410 E. 47th St.
Wrights—3753 S. Wabash Ave.
A & J—105 E. 51st St.
Pitts—812 E. 39th St.
Palm Gardens—720 E. Oakwood Blvd.
400 Club—715 E. 63rd St.
Pioneer—533 E. 43rd St.
Pershing—755 East 64th Street
TOURIST HOMES
DAY'S VISITORS HOME
3616 SO. PARKWAY
Mrs. Ethel M. Day, Mgr.
Mabel Bank—712 E. 44th St.
Poro College—4415 S. Parkway
BEAUTY PARLORS
Mattiee'—4212 Cottage Grove Ave.
BARBER SHOPS
Bank's—209 E. 39th St.

18

What to See in Chicago

Every section of Chicago is served by the Chicago surface lines. Car stops are indicated by White Bands on the poles at street intersections. 98% of the population live within three blocks of one or more surface lines.

Below are listed many of the principal points of interest in Chicago.

AIRPORTS — Chicago Municipal Airport—63rd St. and Cicero Ave. One of the nations finest airports and the greatest scene of aeronautical activity in the United States. Board southbound State St. cars on State St. or Clark-Wentworth or through Route No. 22 cars in Clark St. and transfer West on 63rd St. to Cicero Ave.

AMUSEMENTS

Riverside Park—Belmont and Western Aves. A large summer amusement park. Take Riverview-Larrabee cars at Dearborn and Randolph Sts. or Clybourn Ave. cars at Wells St. direct to park. By transfer north on Western Ave. or west on Belmont Ave. direct to park.

BASEBALL PARKS

Cubs Park (Wrigley Field) Clark and Addison Sts. (1100 W.—3600 N.) Home grounds of the Chicago National League baseball team. Take Clark-Wentworth or through Route No. 22 cars on Clark St. north to main entrance.

White Sox Park (Comiskey Park)

West 35th St. and Shields Ave. Home grounds of the Chicago American League baseball team. Take Clark-Wentworth or through Route No. 22 cars on Clark St., south to 35th St. and Wentworth Ave. Baseball park, one block west.

MANUFACTURING AND INDUSTRIES

Central Manufacturing District — Between Ashland Ave., Morgan St., 35th St. and Pershing Road (1600 W. to 1000 W. and 3500 S. to 3900 S.) Also along Pershing Road between Ashland and Western Aves. This district contains about 250 nationally known manufacturing concerns. Take south bound Ashland Ave. cars on State St. and transfer on 35th St.

Union Stock Yards — Between Pershing Road, 47th St., Halstead St. and S. Ashland Ave. (3900 S. to 4700 S.) (800 W. to 1600 W.) The world's famous center of the packing industry. Take south bound Halstead St. cars on Clark St., or Wallace-Racine Ave. cars on State St. direct to main entrance at Halstead and Root Sts.

MUSEUMS

Chicago Historical Museum — The best collection of American historical mementos are displayed here. Relics of Columbus, Lincoln, Spanish explorers, the French voyageurs and the Indian Northwest are shown. A real education. Admission Free Mondays, Wednesdays and Fridays. Address, in Lincoln Park at Clark St. and North Ave.

Adler Planetarium and Astronomical Museum—Located on Lake Michigan at Roosevelt Road (1200 S.) and open to the public. Demonstrations with lectures at 11 A.M. and 3 P.M. on Monday, Wednesday, Thursday and Saturday. At 11 A.M., 3 and 8 P.M., on Tuesday and Friday; at 3 and 4 P.M. on Sunday. Admission Free on Wednesday, Saturday and Sunday.

19

By 1949, the price of the Green Book had grown along with its size—it cost 75 cents and was 80 pages. It covered all the United States, Bermuda, Mexico, and Canada!

In the 1950s and early 1960s, civil rights leaders like Martin Luther King Jr. brought national and international recognition to the injustices suffered by African Americans. Jim Crow's days were numbered. On July 2, 1964, President Lyndon Johnson signed the Civil Rights Bill into law. Among other things, this act made it illegal for hotels, restaurants, and gas stations to discriminate against customers.

Victor Green published the final edition of the Green Book that same year—1964. His lifelong dream to see African American travelers treated equally was finally a reality.

To view a copy of a real Green Book online, visit www.ruthandthegreenbook.com.